About the Author

Stephen Bibby has won numerous writing awards for short stories and travel articles. Additionally he has published two novels which have received excellent reviews from readers.

Having written several unpublished short stories for his grandchildren, in 2016 he published 'The Cube and the Crew: 2222' especially for them. He has now followed this up with 'The Labours of Heracles' both to entertain Katie, Calder, Harry and Zara and also to tell them more of the wonderful world of Greek mythology than he has managed in bedtime stories.

Copyright

ISBN -13: 978-1729514955

ISBN – 10: 1729514952

Copyright © Stephen Bibby 2018

First Published 2018

The Labours of Heracles

Re-told by

Stephen Bibby

Dedication

To my grandchildren:

Katie Pine

Calder Bibby

Harry Pine

Zara Bibby

Four very special people

The Labours

of

Heracles

Introduction

One of the most famous heroes of ancient Greek mythology was Heracles, although perhaps he is more widely known as 'Hercules'.

There is a simple explanation for this. The ancient Greeks believed that many gods lived on Mount Olympus. They made sacrifices to them and told stories about them. These stories are known as myths. Many of the myths were about heroes. Sometimes these heroes became favourites of certain gods and were helped by them: sometimes they became enemies and were hindered by them.

When the city of Rome was founded in about 750 BC, the Greeks had already been telling and re-telling these myths for many generations. As the Romans became more powerful, they conquered the Greek empire. Over time they learnt about the Greek gods and the many Greek myths. Several Roman writers compiled books recording the stories and, quite understandably, when they did so they changed the Greek names to Latin, the language of ancient Rome.

In Latin Heracles is known as Hercules, the name which has become more familiar. There is a constellation of stars named Hercules. In the 1950s a military transport plane named 'The Hercules' was built. Its name was chosen because it was large and strong enough to carry the heavy equipment used by armies in battle. For hundreds of years Hercules has been the nickname of many a strongman.

However, as the tales which are the subject of this book were originally Greek myths, I have chosen to use the original Greek names. Therefore the hero known to the Romans as Hercules has been given his original Greek name, Heracles.

In the accounts of the Labours of Heracles we meet a number of ancient gods and goddesses. Because some may be better known by their later Roman names, on the next page you will find a list of those who appear in these stories.

Title	Greek Name	Roman Name
King of the gods	Zeus	Jupiter
His wife	Hera	Juno
Goddess of Wisdom	Athene	Minerva
Goddess of Hunting	Artemis	Diana
Blacksmith of the gods	Hephaestus	Vulcan
God of the Sun	Helios	Sol
God of the Underworld	Hades	Pluto
His wife	Persephone	Prosperina
Messenger of the gods	Hermes	Mercury
Old man of the sea	Nereus	Nereus

****

The Baby Heracles

The king of the gods, Zeus, was immortal. He lived through all eternity together with other gods and goddesses on Mount Olympus in Greece.

Like all those who dwelt on Mount Olympus, from time to time Zeus travelled far and wide. He often became involved in the lives of mortals, the ordinary men and women who lived in ancient Greece.

Although Zeus was a god, he sometimes fell in love with beautiful ladies living far away from Mount Olympus. One of his favourites was called Alcmene. Zeus often visited her and eventually she gave birth to a baby who she named Heracles.

As Zeus was his father and a god and as Alcmene was his mother, but mortal, this meant that Heracles was half mortal and half immortal. He could not live for ever like the gods, but he could live longer than ordinary mortal beings and enjoy protection from illness and other dangers.

From the very moment Heracles was born, Athene, goddess of wisdom, smiled upon him. She knew that he would grow up to become famous. She also knew that, even as a baby, Heracles would possess superhuman strength.

One day Athene descended from Mount Olympus with Zeus's wife, Hera. They went for a walk in the warm sunshine through a lovely green meadow. Athene led the way because she knew that Alcmene often allowed Heracles to sleep, lying on the soft, lush grass.

Sure enough before long Athene cried out, pointing to the sleeping baby.

"Look at the poor child," she said. "His mother has left him all alone in a field. He will die if he does not have milk."

Athene knew that several weeks earlier Hera herself had given birth to a baby. Now, feeling sorry for the tiny Heracles, Hera bent down, picked him up and allowed him to suckle at her breast.

She did not realise that this innocent child was ferociously strong. With his infant lips Heracles tugged so hard that he drew the milk with a great rush. This caused Hera so much pain that, shocked and surprised, she flung this extraordinary baby away from her. But still the milk shot from her breast into a great fountain soaring up into the heavens. There it separated into tiny drops and stayed for ever in the night sky. It is known to us today as the belt of stars named the Milky Way.

Until this point Heracles had not been immortal. But at that moment, because his father had been a god and he had now tasted the milk of a goddess, Heracles achieved everlasting life.

Hera herself was in terrible pain. She cried out, clutching her sore breast. In that moment she developed a feeling of the deepest hate for the baby Heracles. For evermore she would be his enemy.

Once she had returned to Mount Olympus, Hera plotted her revenge. The more she thought about it, the more she resolved to destroy Heracles. But she faced one enormous problem. Heracles was now immortal.

Only gods or goddesses, not ordinary people, had the power to harm someone immortal. Even so, Hera had to think carefully about how she could attack the baby Heracles. This was difficult because she knew he was watched over constantly by Alcmene.

Eventually Hera devised a fiendishly wicked plan. In the dead of night she sent two enormous serpents to the house of Alcmene. She charmed them so that in a deathly trance they made their way directly to the room where

Heracles lay sleeping in a cradle with his baby brother, Iphicles.

Silently, the serpents slithered across the courtyard, under the doorway and across the marble floors. Rapidly they glided into the nursery, their eyes shooting flames, evil poison dripping from their fearsome fangs.

The scaly serpents hissed as their heads reared up above the babies' cradle. With a start the sleeping infants awoke in horror to see huge, forked tongues flicking into their faces. Instantly they yelled out, screaming as loudly as their tiny lungs would permit.

Alcmene came running at top speed, clutching a flaming torch. What she saw amazed her.

Heracles was sitting by his brother clutching one writhing serpent in each hand. With his baby arms he was wrestling with both the scaly creatures sent to strangle him. They slithered across his chest and around his chubby wrists, but he simply squeezed harder and harder. As Alcmene watched, the breath was choked out of the serpents until they fell limp and lifeless onto the floor.

With utter astonishment Alcmene realised that the baby Heracles was stronger than any man. From that moment she knew he would grow up able to perform tremendous feats. She realised that her child possessed the unique gift of stupendous strength.

Heracles Made Mad

Because he was such a strong man, Heracles became an excellent soldier. He fought in many battles, often winning them by himself because others were easily felled by the power of his mighty muscles.

Hera, watching from Mount Olympus, grew more and more angry. She would never forgive Heracles for the pain he had inflicted on her when he was a tiny baby. Hera had failed to destroy him, but in a cunning and evil plan, she decided to drive him mad.

This was a truly terrible time for Heracles. Out of his mind, he simply did not know what he was doing. In one rage of madness, he viciously attacked and killed his children. Wrongly thinking they were enemies, Heracles shot them with his arrows before throwing their bodies onto a fire.

When, finally, the mad episode passed, Heracles was horrified by what he had done and desperately upset. He shut himself away in a dark room for several days, not talking to anyone at all. He had no idea what to do with his life.

After a long time, when once more he could think clearly, Heracles decided that he would travel to the city of Delphi. There he would visit the Oracle and ask for guidance.

The Oracle at Delphi was famous in the ancient Greek world. It was a temple where the priestess gave prophecies or advice.

Heracles walked into the dark temple, his head bowed. The priestess was seated behind a constantly curling cloud of smoke, veiling her from onlookers. With great sadness Heracles told her what had happened.

There was a long silence.

Eventually, from behind the swirls of smoke, Heracles heard the sing-song voice of the priestess. As if in a trance, she announced that to obtain peace Heracles should atone for the terrible things he had done. Still hidden and speaking with a strange chant, she directed him to travel to the land of King Eurystheus and once there to perform whatever tasks he was given.

Heracles did as he was told. After a long journey he presented himself to King Eurystheus and told his sorry tale.

The king listened carefully then said to Heracles, "I will give you ten tasks. Carry these out and return to me with proof that you have done what I commanded and you will be forgiven."

These tasks have become famous the world over. They are known as the 'Labours of Heracles'.

The First Labour - The Nemean Lion

Near the town of Nemea lived an enormous lion. It was a vicious beast which caused havoc in the surrounding countryside. The lion would come out of its cave to attack and eat any person unfortunate enough to fall into its path.

Many people had tried to kill the lion but had died in the attempt. The creature was simply too strong for them. They did not realise that all weapons would fail as the lion's skin was tougher than even the strongest shield. No one knew that the hairy hide could not be damaged in any way: not by fire, metal or stone.

King Eurystheus commanded Heracles to travel to Nemea. Once there he was to find the lion, kill it and bring back its skin to prove that he had carried out the task.

Heracles set off on a long journey. Once he reached Nemea he asked anyone he met where he could find the lion's den. But there were very few people who could tell him as most of those who dwelt nearby had been attacked and killed by the fearsome beast.

Instead, Heracles began to search a wide area of countryside. At last, on a bare mountainside amongst large rocks and boulders, he spotted several caves. Near the entrance to one of these he spied a heap of strange white shapes. Looking more closely, he saw they were scattered human bones and shattered skulls. Heracles had found the lion's lair.

Crouching behind a large rock, Heracles remained hidden all day. At last, towards nightfall, the lion appeared.

As soon as the creature was within range, Heracles fired off a rapid flight of arrows. They sang with a high-pitched hum as they shot through the air. His aim was perfect. The arrows flew directly at the lion's flank. But when they hit, they simply bounced off. The lion's skin was so tough that even speeding arrows could not penetrate it.

The snarling beast turned towards Heracles. It now appeared even more evil. Its slavering mouth was covered in blood, still dripping, as it had feasted well that day on yet more unfortunate citizens of Nemea.

Fearing he would become the lion's next meal, Heracles charged. He held his sword straight out, stretching his stout arm, and thrust with all his might. But to his shock, Heracles saw his weapon bend. It crumpled when it hit the lion's skin as if it were not made of hardened bronze but of lead, one of the softest of all the metals known to man.

Heracles was becoming desperate. He swung the enormous wooden club which he always carried, his sinews taut as he delivered a mighty blow to the lion's head. The weapon simply split on contact with the solid skull. But the force of the blow sent the lion roaring into its cave, angrily shaking its huge mane. It had not felt the slightest pain but had been driven into a fury by an almighty ringing sound in its ears as the club cracked to pieces.

But the lion of Nemea had made a huge mistake. It did not know that Heracles had already discovered the cave. Neither did it know that Heracles had also looked carefully and spotted that the cave possessed two entrances. As soon as the lion had retreated inside, Heracles stretched a huge net over one mouth of the cave. He then crept inside through the other entrance.

Slowly, Heracles made his way into the depths of the dark cavern, carefully stepping over boulders and broken bones. He heard the sound of the lion's breathing long before he saw it. He knew the beast would be crouching, waiting for the right moment to pounce upon its attacker.

With a mighty snarl, the lion bounded to its feet, roared and charged. Realising that his weapons were useless, Heracles stretched out his powerful hands. As the huge tough hide and hairy mane crashed down upon him, Heracles grasped the throat of the charging creature and pressed as hard as he could on its thick windpipe.

An almighty wrestling contest began. The lion roared and writhed, but Heracles courageously clung on. He cried with pain as the lion bit off one of his fingers. But he was determined he would win. He crushed the lion's neck with tremendous pressure, just as he had crushed the necks of Hera's serpents when he was a babe.

Slowly the lion's coarse breathing began to fade away. Its body fell limp and slumped to Heracles' feet, choked to death.

To complete this Labour Heracles knew he was required to strip off the thick skin from the lion and carry it back to King Eurystheus. He drew his knife along the belly of the beast but found it made not so much as a scratch. Like his sword before, his knife was useless against the hide which was as hard as granite.

Heracles spent several hours wondering how to complete his task. Finding no solution to the problem and tired out, he eventually fell asleep. While he was dreaming he was visited by the goddess Athene.

Athene had always favoured Heracles, in contrast to the goddess Hera who had always disliked him. Now, in the depths of his slumbers, Athene whispered softly into his ear and an idea took root in his mind.

When he awoke, Heracles turned to the lion's body nearby. He grabbed the beast's foreleg, bent it towards its stomach and used one of the animal's razor sharp claws as a knife. Immediately it cut through the tough hide.

Handling the claw like a sheep-shearer's knife, Heracles removed the thick mane. In the same way he peeled back the entire skin. Then he wrapped both the lion's mane and its hide into a bundle and started his long journey back to the court of King Eurystheus.

The king was amazed that the ferocious lion had been killed and pleased that the people of Nemea were safe. Yet he was also terrified. He never thought that Heracles would succeed and now became very afraid. Eurystheus now realised how much strength Heracles possessed. Being a suspicious man, he feared that one day Heracles might attack him and that he would immediately be defeated by someone so powerful.

King Eurystheus issued two very strict orders. Firstly he decreed that in future Heracles was never to enter his city. Secondly he required his blacksmiths to cast a huge urn made of bronze. After this, whenever Eurystheus was told Heracles was approaching, he hid himself inside the urn to make sure that he would always be completely safe.

But this cowardly king said nothing about the bundle which had been brought back to him. Once he was alone, Heracles unwrapped it. He decided that he would drape himself in the tough skin of the lion which for ever after acted like a suit of armour and protected him during many other adventures.

The Second Labour - The Lernean Hydra

If you were ever unfortunate enough to meet Hera you would very soon decide she was a deeply unpleasant goddess. She was forever thinking of ways to destroy whatever she hated. In her plotting and planning she created a monster which she imagined not even the mighty Heracles would be able to overcome. This terrifying creature was known as the Hydra. It lived in a deep cave near the town of Lerna.

The Hydra had an enormous body shaped like that of a huge dog. But, rearing up from its neck was no dog's nose, eyes and ears, but nine huge serpent heads. Each head held narrow eyes and a forked tongue. If you ever felt the breath coming from the Hydra, you would instantly know it was the most deadly, gaseous poison. It immediately killed any person or beast who inhaled it.

The single-handed destruction of this weird and terrifying creature was the next Labour ordered by King Eurystheus.

Heracles travelled to Lerna in a chariot driven by his nephew, Iolaus. When he arrived, once again the goddess Athene helped him. Firstly, she pointed out where the Hydra was hiding, deep in its lair. Then she gave some very wise advice.

Heracles listened carefully to the friendly goddess and, based on what she suggested, devised a plan. He would force the Hydra to leave its cave by shooting burning arrows inside. When the Hydra appeared, he would protect himself by wrapping his face in thick cloth so that he would not inhale the monster's poisonous breath.

Once Heracles put his plan into action, the Hydra leapt from its cave and immediately attacked him. It wound one of its long serpent necks around Heracles' right leg, trying to topple him over. Swinging his new and even heavier club with great force, Heracles knocked the deadly head off the entwining body. But before it had hit the ground two fresh heads sprang up to take its place.

Yet again a serpent neck reared up menacingly. This time in a vicious whipping action, it wound itself around Heracles' left leg. Again Heracles lopped off the head with a mighty blow from his club: again two new heads promptly sprouted up, taking the place of the bloodied mess lying on the ground.

Moments later, an enormous crab crawled out of a nearby swamp to help the Hydra. With its gigantic claw it nipped Heracles' foot causing him to cry out in pain. He stamped heavily upon this unwelcome assailant, crushing its pink shell into small pieces, just before another snaking neck shot out at him.

Heracles did not know it, but the crab had been sent by Hera. Aware that Athene was advising Heracles, she had commanded the crustacean, with its enormous pincers, to help the Hydra. It obeyed and assisted the multi-headed monster by distracting Heracles at a vital moment. As a reward for its services Hera set the image of the crab in the night sky as a constellation, 'Cancer the Crab'. Today it is still one of the twelve signs of the Zodiac.

Heracles battled bravely against a growing number of hissing serpent heads. Even with his great strength he began to tire and to realise that he could not defeat the Hydra unless he tried a new tactic. Desperately he called out to Iolaus.

Doing as Heracles asked, Iolaus set fire to a nearby grove of trees which were soon crackling and burning fiercely. Now, every time a head was sent flying from the Hydra's body, Iolaus handed Heracles a blazing branch. Before a new head could grow, Heracles thrust the red-hot branch into the severed neck, searing the blood vessels and preventing any further spitting serpents from emerging.

As Heracles continued his long battle with the Hydra, he noticed that among the writhing serpent heads was one that appeared to dominate all the rest. This head shone and sparkled because it was partly covered in gold. Heracles realised that this had to be his target.

Putting down his club, Heracles reached for his sword, a fine razor sharp weapon also made of gold. With an almighty swing it curved through the air, severing the golden head at its root. Immediately Heracles seized the head, still hissing with poisonous breath, and thrust it deep into the ground so it could do no further damage.

The body of the Hydra now lay crumpled and collapsed. Its severed necks lay in a pool of blood spreading out from its massive dog-like body. Once the monster had stopped twitching and Heracles was sure it was dead, he cut it open and dipped his arrows into the foul acid in its stomach. From that day forward a wound from his arrows would be instantly fatal to any person or creature they hit.

After a well-earned rest, Heracles and Iolaus travelled back to King Eurystheus to give a full account of what had happened. They both thought the king would be astonished to hear of the almighty battle with the Hydra and pleased that the monster had been destroyed.

Instead, Eurystheus was furious. He ranted at Heracles, shouting at him that he had not done what had been commanded. He repeated that all the tasks had to be carried out single-handed.

Because Heracles had received help from Iolaus, King Eurystheus inwardly decided that this Labour should not count as a task that had been carried out properly.

The Third Labour - The Ceryneian Hind

The goddess Hera was becoming increasingly angry. Heracles had now survived two Labours despite her attempts to thwart him.

Secretly visiting King Eurystheus, she persuaded him that the next task for Heracles should be the capture of a very special female deer, known as the Ceryneian Hind.

What made the Ceryneian Hind stand out was her fine appearance. She possessed graceful hooves of bronze and fine golden horns, as proud as any that ever adorned the most handsome stag. This wondrous creature belonged to the goddess Artemis. As a child Artemis had seen five such hinds grazing peacefully. She claimed ownership of all five, but one had escaped from her and now lived on a mountain known as the Ceryneian Hill.

Heracles was ordered to bring the hind alive and unharmed to King Eurystheus. Hera had planned this, thinking it would be an impossible task. She knew that the hind would struggle if captured. She fully expected that Heracles, with his mighty strength, would cause some injury to the beautiful animal as he tried to subdue her. She also knew that if any injury were inflicted upon the hind Artemis would be furious and would take her revenge on Heracles.

For one whole year Heracles hunted the hind. He pursued her through the length and breadth of Greece. At last the hind was worn out and lay down by a river to drink. Heracles spied her there and, with deadly accuracy, fired an arrow. As he intended, the arrow pinned the hind's two front legs together. His aim had been so careful that the arrow passed between bones and sinews and drew no blood. He had also been careful to choose an arrow not tipped with poison. The hind was disabled but unharmed.

Heracles promptly tied her up, slung her across his shoulders and started the long journey back to King Eurystheus.

The goddess Artemis, looking down from Mount Olympus, spotted Heracles carrying the Cerynian Hind. She was furious because the beautiful creature which she claimed as her own had been captured and carried away. In a rage she appeared before Heracles.

Immediately Heracles sank to his knees, giving great respect to Artemis. Firstly, he showed her that the hind was not injured. Then he told her all the details of his life. Sorrowfully, he outlined the terrible things he had done while in his fit of madness. He was bitterly sorry for his deeds and determined to carry out the ten Labours to atone for them.

Artemis listened. The sad tale touched her heart and tears sprang from her eyes. Forgiving Heracles, she allowed him to carry the hind to King Eurystheus as he had been ordered.

Yet again Hera had been unable to hinder Heracles and the task assigned to him was successfully completed.

The Fourth Labour - The Erymantian Boar

King Eurystheus was shocked to discover that Heracles had found the Ceryneian Hind. He was even more shocked to discover he had brought it back uninjured.

He now thought up an even greater challenge. For his fourth Labour King Eurystheus required Heracles to capture alive an enormous, fierce wild boar which lived on the slopes of Mount Erymanthus.

Yet again Heracles set off, this time to travel to the mountain. On the way he visited an old friend, the centaur Pholus. Centaurs were strange creatures, having the head, chest and arms of men but the body and legs of horses.

Pholus set roast meat in front of Heracles although he himself ate everything raw. He was reluctant to offer Heracles wine because it was held in one large pitcher which belonged to all the centaurs who lived nearby. However, Heracles persuaded him that it would be enjoyable to drink wine with the meat. Pholus, wishing to be a good host to his visitor, reached for the pitcher, removed the large lid and filled a drinking goblet.

The wine was very strong and the rich smell of it quickly wafted across the mountainside. All the other centaurs came rushing to the cave and they too demanded wine. They guzzled it down rapidly and soon became very drunk. Staggering about unsteadily, they started shouting and arguing. Then a huge fight broke out. The centaurs all began attacking Heracles saying he had no right to drink wine which was their property. Heracles was forced to defend himself and shot several centaurs with his poisoned arrows.

The rest ran off and hid in a cave which was the home of a centaur called Cheiron. Unfortunately, in the fighting Cheiron was accidentally wounded by one of the arrows. He was in terrible pain but he did not die because he was immortal and so there was no release from his suffering.

Cheiron realised that his injury was an accident. He looked kindly upon Heracles and wanted to help him. Even though his wound gave him agony, he managed to explain to Heracles the only possible way to capture the Erymantian Boar.

Following Cheiron's advice, Heracles travelled onwards to Mount Erymanthus. It was the middle of winter and no leaves were on the trees. But the boar could still hide and concealed itself in a dense thicket. Heracles yelled at it loudly so that the beast became alarmed. It ran out of its hiding place and into a very deep snowdrift. It was so huge and heavy that it sank down into the great bank of cold, soft whiteness. It used all its energy to flee from Heracles but on four legs it could not move quickly through the snow and struggled unsuccessfully to escape.

Heracles chased after it, carry him large coils of stout chains in his strong, sinewy arms. With an enormous leap into the snowdrift, he came down heavily onto the boar's rough back, pinning it to the ground. He quickly wrapped the heavy chains around the legs of the boar so it could move no more. With an almighty heave, he lifted the hobbled creature and slung it over his shoulders.

Heracles could now return to King Eurystheus. He made the long journey on foot, carrying upon his broad back the Erymantian Boar, alive, uninjured and bound with chains.

King Eurystheus was warned by his courtiers that Heracles was returning. Afraid of coming face to face with a vicious beast, he hid himself inside his bronze urn. From there this timid king shouted out an echoing command. Although he had ordered that the boar be brought back alive, he was so afraid that he now commanded that it should immediately be put to death.

The Fifth Labour - The Augean Stables

King Eurystheus took a secret pleasure in planning tasks which he thought Heracles would find impossible. Having been terrified at the appearance of the Erymantian Boar, he now decided that Heracles should be given a task which was quite disgusting.

He sent him to visit King Augeias who was the owner of a huge herd of cattle. More than 1,000 magnificent bulls, cows and calves lived in the king's huge stable block. For over 30 years the stables had never been cleaned out. There was hardly room to move inside them because of the heaps of stinking animal dung that were growing ever taller and wider. It was difficult for anyone to go near the stables because the stench was overpowering.

The task set by King Eurystheus was for Heracles to clean the stables in a single day.

Again Heracles travelled with his nephew, Iolaus, for company. Reaching the kingdom of Augeias, Heracles could smell for himself the terrible, sickening stink coming from the stables. Knowing he had only one day in which to carry out his task, he devised a clever plan.

He arranged to meet King Augeias in a place where they could talk without being overcome by the foul smell. They stood on a spot overlooking the stables, mid way between two rivers.

"I am prepared to do some important work for you," said Heracles. "Would you like me to clean out these filthy stables?"

"Of course," replied the king.

"Very well," responded Heracles. "But as you see, it is a huge job. If I can complete the work in one day will you reward me by giving me one tenth of the cattle?"

"Complete the work in one day!" King Augeias laughed loudly. "If you do that you shall certainly have your tenth."

But Augeias thought to himself that there was no possibility of that happening.

Heracles rose very early the next morning and went to the stables, taking Iolaus with him. Helped by his nephew, he made a large gap in each end wall.

After this, he marched firstly to the bank of one nearby river and then another. He dug with all his might and by late afternoon had made channels from each of the rivers leading directly to the fresh gaps in the wall of the stables. Just as the day was ending and night was beginning to fall, Heracles dug out the final clods of earth between channel and river. The water came rushing down the canals he had created and into the stables.

A huge wall of raging river water poured through the middle of the stables. Such was its force that in an instant it swept away the huge mounds of stinking cow dung. The stables were completely clean.

The next day Heracles went to King Augeais and demanded one tenth of all the cattle, as had been agreed. But, unknown to Heracles, during the night a messenger had arrived. From him King Augeais learnt that Heracles had been commanded to carry out the unpleasant cleaning work as one of the tasks set by King Eurystheus. He needed to do it whether or not he was rewarded. King Augeais therefore refused to give Heracles what had been agreed and sent him back to Eurystheus.

When Heracles returned, King Eurystheus considered that yet again a Labour had not been properly carried out. This was both because Heracles had tried to obtain payment and because he had not done the work alone, having received some help from Iolaus.

The Sixth Labour - The Stymphalian Birds

Heracles was next sent by King Eurystheus to the River Stymphalia. He was ordered to rid the area of a flock of man-eating birds which were causing great terror to all those who lived nearby.

After travelling to the river, Heracles reached a low-lying spot where the waters merged with the surrounding land to create an enormous marsh. It was not so wet that you could sail a boat upon it, but neither was it so dry that you could easily walk through it. Instead, if you stepped into the sticky mud you were likely to become trapped, unable to escape from its cloying grasp.

The marsh was home to the huge flock of fearsome birds which Heracles was commanded to remove. From a distance the Stymphalain Birds resembled storks, but when they flew you could see that their beaks, claws and even their wings were made of bronze. They were vicious creatures. If they were hungry they would soar away from the marsh, swooping down over the countryside, snatching both men and cattle which they carried off to eat.

This was not the only menace. To make matters worse, their droppings were poisonous. As they flew over the land all the crops beneath became ruined by the sticky, stinking, mess falling from these armoured and aggressive birds.

Heracles decided he needed to get close to the enormous flock to be able to hit the birds with his arrows. But, hesitantly setting foot on the edge of the marsh, he realised it was impossible to walk through it. As he could not take a boat there seemed to be no way in which he could approach.

He walked away, scratching his head in puzzlement, and sat down upon a large rock looking out over the marsh. He put down his bow and arrows and wondered what to do, fearing that this was a Labour he would be unable to carry out.

Suddenly, while he was still sitting lost in thought, a beautiful lady appeared at his side. She was the goddess Athene. She had always looked kindly upon Heracles and now came to his rescue.

From the folds of her cloak she produced a gift. It was something simple but very special, having been made for Athene, at her request, by one of the other gods, Hephaestus.

Hephaestus was the blacksmith of the gods. He was the owner of a wondrous forge, hidden deep inside Mount Olympus. After he had been approached by the beautiful Athene, Hephaestus descended into the mountain and stoked the fire of his forge until it glowed bright red. Then he heated a piece of metal in a cauldron. Reaching a very high temperature, it became molten and Hephaestus poured it onto his anvil. Hammering quickly and carefully, he shaped a pair of beautiful bronze castanets.

It was these shiny, chiming instruments which Athene handed to Heracles. He rose to take them and as soon as the castanets passed from her outstretched hands, the goddess disappeared.

After thinking for a moment Heracles knew exactly what he had to do. Raising his arms, he waved the castanets violently, making an almighty noise. This terrified the birds standing in the marsh. Like normal birds when they are shocked and scared, the Stymphalian Birds took to the air in a mad frenzy, squawking loudly and madly flapping their bronze wings which crashed and clattered, adding to the dreadful din.

Heracles immediately seized his bow and arrows. He fired rapidly, one arrow after another, until most of the birds had fallen, flopping down in a clattering spiral to be swallowed up by the treacherous marsh. He had successfully completed another Labour.

All the birds had been cleared away from the River Stymphalia and most of them killed. But a few escaped. They flew away to a distant island where they were discovered some years later by another ancient Greek hero named Jason, during his famous voyage with the Argonauts.

The Seventh Labour - The Cretan Bull

The island of Crete was menaced by an enormous bull. It was a truly terrifying creature. When it charged, heavy and lumbering, the earth shook. From its large, snorting nose and mouth it belched out scorching flames.

For his next Labour, King Eurystheus ordered Heracles to sail to Crete and to capture the bull single-handed.

After a voyage by sea, Heracles was met by the ruler of Crete, King Minos. The king desperately wished to see the bull destroyed or at least carried away from the island. It was causing great devastation and bringing misery to his people. He therefore greeted Heracles joyfully and offered him all possible help.

Heracles did not wish to be rude, but politely refused the offer. He was now very worried that if he accepted any assistance the task would not be counted as having been completed by him single-handed. He had no wish to anger King Eurystheus even more and decided to set off alone in search of the bull.

It was not difficult to find the rampaging creature. Heracles quickly spotted where the bull had trampled over the growing crops. Wheat fields had been flattened by its clumsy, heavy hooves. Orchards had been wrecked by its wild charging in search of fruit, the trees blackened by its fiery breath.

Heracles found the monstrous animal, snorting and stamping, a few feet away from a wall. The bull's head was lowered menacingly. It was ready to charge.

Reaching swiftly for his arrows, at the last minute Heracles remembered his instructions. He had been commanded to capture the bull and take it back alive to King Eurystheus. Despite his excellent skill as a bowman, Heracles knew it would be unwise to fire arrows. If the bull charged, as he expected, it could be stopped only by an arrow, but that could do more damage than intended and even prove fatal.

Instead, very quietly, and keeping out of sight, Heracles carefully made his way around to the back of the wall. He stole silently along it until he was behind the bull, whose snorting and snuffling indicated where it was standing. Nimbly, Heracles vaulted over the wall and, step by step, crept up behind the angry creature.

Standing directly behind the beast's enormous rump, Heracles flexed the large muscles in his arms. Then, taking a gigantic leap, he grasped the snorting monster around its neck. The bull kicked, stamped and jerked its huge head violently from side to side. Heracles squeezed tighter and tighter, clinging on with great determination despite the beast's frantic attempts to throw him off. With sweat pouring off him, Heracles firmly held his steely grip, throttling the bull until it crumpled unconscious at his feet.

Only now did Heracles release the creature for a moment. Snatching a rope, he bound the bull's legs and, with an almighty heave, slung it over his back. Unaided, staggering slightly under the weight, Heracles carried the beast, its legs trussed, its jaw tied firmly shut, down to the harbour. Using more ropes and pulleys, the bull was hoisted on board his ship and Heracles set sail on the voyage back to King Eurystheus.

On hearing of Heracles' arrival, King Eurystheus once again hid in his bronze urn. He was growing more afraid of Heracles and was terrified of the fearsome bull.

From inside the urn he shouted out, his words sounding like a ringing bell, 'Take this monstrous beast to the temple. It shall be a sacrifice to the great goddess Hera.'

But Hera, who had always hated Heracles, ordered the priests in the temple to refuse the sacrifice. She could not bear to see Heracles succeed and certainly would not accept the sacrifice of a beast he had captured using his amazing strength.

Instead the Cretan bull was set free. It was driven out of the land. For many years it roamed the countryside causing destruction wherever it went, until finally it settled near the city named Marathon. Years later another ancient Greek hero, Theseus, found and slew the creature on his way to Crete to encounter a similar monster known as the Minotaur.

The Eighth Labour - The Mares of Diomedes

On the border of Greece and Turkey was a kingdom known as Thrace. Its ruler was King Diomedes.

This king was known throughout the ancient world as a wicked man. He often treated people he disliked in a horribly cruel manner and became widely feared and hated.

King Diomedes owned four savage mares. These creatures were terrifying. They were so wild and vicious that they were kept locked in a stable, firmly tethered with iron chains anchoring them onto a heavy bronze manger. If any visitors upset Diomedes he had them taken to the stable and fed to the hungry horses. Normal horses eat only hay and grass and are known as herbivores. But these savage animals belonging to Diomedes were different. They ate flesh and so were carnivores.

For his eighth Labour King Eurystheus ordered Heracles to travel to Thrace, find and then capture the Mares of Diomedes.

Yet again Heracles made a long voyage by sea. He had heard all about Diomedes and was not looking forward to meeting him. Rightly believing that this evil king would never simply hand over his horses, Heracles spent some time aboard ship devising a plan.

Once Thrace had come into sight, Heracles issued an order to the ship's captain to sail into a quiet bay. There, in the dead of night, he waded to the shore. Hidden by the darkness, he crept up to the stable where the mares were kept and looked around. Two grooms were standing guard, but Heracles easily overpowered them.

He stepped inside the stable where he could hear the fierce mares neighing menacingly. Quickly he seized their iron tethering chains in both hands, pulling them apart so they snapped like brittle brushwood. Such was his strength that in an instant Heracles had released the mares.

Now he had to think quickly. Heracles feared that as soon as Diomedes was told that the mares had escaped he would come chasing after them. With this in mind Heracles set off, driving the beasts towards the sea where his ship was moored. But the vicious animals kicked and reared and were so difficult to control that the journey was slower then Heracles had reckoned. He knew that Diomedes would quickly catch up with him.

Before reaching the shore, Heracles came to a small hill. Turning from his path, he forced the animals up onto the low summit, taking with him a companion, Abderus who had been on the ship with him. Abderus was given the task of guarding the mares.

With the mares secured, Heracles could turn and face Diomedes. As dawn broke he looked down from the hilltop. A cloud of dust in the distance indicated that not only was Diomedes driving in his chariot towards him, but also that he was leading a small army. Although brave and strong, Heracles knew he could not overcome an entire army single handed. He thought carefully about what to do next.

With sudden inspiration, drawing on all his reserves of strength, Heracles immediately set to work. At a furious pace, barely pausing for breath, he dug a channel from the foot of the hill to the sea. As soon as the channel reached the tide line the waves rolled in and flooded the plain.

Diomedes and his army, shaken and surprised, were halted by this great lake of water. They stood at the far side shouting in anger because they could not reach Heracles.

Thinking that his work was done, Heracles returned to the hilltop. When he arrived he was shocked by what he saw. While he had been away the ferocious mares had turned on Abderus and eaten him alive.

Heracles was deeply upset that the brutal beasts had taken the life of his shipmate. Tying up the mares, he rushed down the hillside again. The soldiers from the army sent to fight him had turned away but Heracles pursued them. He was so strong that he could easily swim across the lake he had created. Reaching the other side, he caught up with King Diomedes who had lingered behind his soldiers. With an almighty blow of his club Heracles stunned Diomedes then carried him back through the lake and up to the hilltop.

Even though it might have been deserved, the fate Heracles inflicted upon Diomedes was terrible. Still angry at the death of Abderus, Heracles threw Diomedes to the mares who immediately ripped him to pieces. He had become food for his own horses.

Finally Heracles hitched the mares to the chariot captured from Diomedes as this was the best way of keeping them under control. Seizing the reins, he drove the beasts furiously. To ensure the mares did not escape and were held permanently between the shafts of the chariot, Heracles decided to travel overland back to the court of King Eurystheus. There, in an act which must have seemed insulting to Heracles, Eurystheus ordered that the mares be dedicated to Hera. He commanded that they be set free in her honour on Mount Olympus.

The Ninth Labour - Hippolyta's Girdle

In a land near the Black Sea, which lies north of present day Turkey, lived a tribe of warriors. They were fierce people: brave, athletic and very warlike. In battle they carried bows made of bronze and short shields shaped like a half-moon. But there was one thing which made them stand out from all other warriors. They were women.

They called themselves Amazons. Their leader was Hippolyta, known as Queen of the Amazons.

To show her status as queen, Hippolyta wore a golden girdle. This was a beautiful broad belt which gleamed brightly in the sunlight. It was envied by anyone who saw it.

The golden girdle was famous throughout ancient Greece. Everyone knew about it, including King Eurystheus. In turn he had described it to his daughter, a rather unpleasant young lady named Admete. The more she thought about it, the more Admete coveted the girdle. She demanded that it should be taken from Hippolyta and constantly pestered her father, stamping her feet and whining annoyingly when she did not get what she wanted.

Eurystheus at last gave in to his tiresome daughter. For the ninth Labour the king ordered Heracles to bring Hippolyta's girdle as a gift for Admete.

Without complaint, once more Heracles set off. Taking some companions with him by ship, he sailed to the land of the Amazons.

When the ship arrived Heracles ordered that it should be anchored a little way from the shore. He knew the reputation of the warlike Amazons and did not wish the ship's crew to face an angry attack.

The Amazons lined the beach and stared out at the strange vessel which had arrived at their land. Hippolyta herself decided she would wade out to the ship to enquire about the purpose of the visit. She strode through the shallow waves without fear because, like other Amazons, she did not think very much of men. Boarding the ship alone, she was well prepared for a fight to the death.

But as soon as she saw Heracles her mood changed. Her eyes fell on his great, strong body, full of mighty muscles. He stood tall, confident and brave, although she detected an air of sadness in him. Immediately she felt a tremendous attraction towards him. She was smitten with love. Without being asked, she promptly removed her magnificent golden girdle and handed it to Heracles as a token of her feelings.

Unknown to Hippolyta, while she was on board the ship the goddess Hera appeared in disguise to the other Amazons. She mingled with the warriors who were waiting on the shore, pretending she was an Amazon herself. Moving quickly, she whispered into one ear and then another. She pointed out that Hippolyta was still on the ship; she suggested that the sailors were preparing to leave. The disguised Hera soon frightened the Amazons into believing that Heracles had captured Queen Hippolyta and was about to carry her off to a distant land.

This rumour quickly spread. Anxiety turned to anger. Encouraged by Hera, the fierce warriors rushed down the beach and started to attack the ship.

Seeing the charging women, yelling with blood curdling cries, brandishing spears and swords, Heracles feared he had been tricked. As the first of the warriors reached the side of the ship, Heracles grabbed his sword. Swinging it mightily, he drove it into Hippolyta's body, killing her instantly.

He called out to his men who hurriedly leapt to his defence. They seized their weapons, hacking at the Amazons climbing up the ropes as they attempted to board the ship. An almighty battle broke out which continued until finally the Amazons fled in defeat.

Shaken by this terrible and sudden battle, Heracles ordered the crew to set sail without delay. After a swift voyage they once more reached the court of King Eurystheus.

This time when Heracles returned the king had no need to hide in his bronze urn. Unlike the fearsome creatures captured in earlier Labours, the golden girdle could do no harm. Eurystheus was seated on his throne with Admete beside him.

"I have done what I was commanded" Heracles cried, handing the golden girdle to the spoilt princess.

Admete grasped it and secured it around her waist, gloating with pride. To her dying day this vain and selfish princess had no idea of the terrible things that had taken place to bring her what she desired.

The Tenth Labour – The Cattle of Geryon

For his next task King Eurystheus commanded Heracles to capture the cattle belonging to King Geryon.

Geryon, King of Tartessus in Spain, was the strangest of men. He had been born with three heads, six hands and three bodies joined together at the waist. Each individual body was very powerful. Thus, although Geryon was only one person, he had as much strength as three men.

King Geryon kept his cattle on the island of Erytheia, the site of what is now Cadiz in Spain. This meant that, to find them, Heracles needed to travel in a westerly direction. The journey was long and difficult. Day after day Heracles trudged his way across the Libyan Desert suffering from the blazing heat. He became so frustrated that he seized his bow and shot an arrow high into the air, directly at the scorching sun. This angered Helios, the sun god, who shouted at him in rage. Immediately Heracles dropped to his knees, uttered a prayer of apology and unstrung his bow.

The sight of this penitent, kneeling traveller, addressing him with utmost courtesy, impressed Helios.

His heart was touched with pity and he decided he would help Heracles. He lent him a large golden goblet shaped like a waterlily. Instead of continuing his tiring trudge across the desert, using this goblet as a vessel, Heracles was able to launch himself into the Mediterranean Sea and then sail to the island of Erytheia.

The winds and the waves carried Heracles, in the goblet, to the point where a narrow passage of water separates the Mediterranean Sea from the Atlantic Ocean. Today this is known as the Straits of Gibraltar. Heracles decided that he would make the straits narrower to discourage whales and other sea monsters from leaving the wild Atlantic and swimming through the gap into the Mediterranean. He built two enormous pillars, one on each side of the narrow gap. It is said that the present Rock of Gibraltar is the northern pillar. To this day the Coat of Arms of Spain contains two pillars which are known as The Pillars of Hercules (using the Roman name).

Once Heracles landed at Erytheia he was met by Geryon's guard dog, a fierce two-headed hound named Orthrus. The creature rushed at him, barking furiously. Heracles swung his heavy club and, with two blows, one at each head, bludgeoned the creature lifeless.

The herdsman guarding the cattle had been roused by the noise. He came running after Orthrus but met the same fate. Heracles struck him down with another blow from his massive club.

Once Geryon learnt of the death of both his two-headed dog, and his herdsman, he was furious. Not trusting anyone else, he decided to go immediately in person to check on his cattle. As soon as he saw Heracles he yelled out, challenging him to stand and fight.

To any normal person Geryon would have been a terrifying opponent. He charged at Heracles, running at full speed, his three heads purple with fury, his six arms reaching out from his three bodies clutching three swords and three spears.

But Heracles was as clever as he was strong. Instead of standing to face Geryon, he ran to one side of him. Then he spun on his heels and let fly an arrow which sped from his bow with tremendous force. Instead of aiming directly at the three flailing bodies, Heracles shot the arrow into Geryon's side. Here it hit, just below Geryon's first rib cage. It did not stop, but continued on its swift passage. The shot was so powerful that the arrow passed directly through Geryon's first body, beyond into the second and came to rest in the stomach of the third.

The goddess Hera, always anxious to make trouble for Heracles, now came rushing to the aid of Geryon. But she was too late. Geryon had already fallen. Seeing Hera kneeling by the stricken king, Heracles let fly another arrow. It hit her on the chest.

Although Hera was immortal she could still feel pain. She yelled out, clutching her wound. Stumbling and hindered by her injury, she was unable to prevent Heracles from escaping.

It took a very long time indeed for Heracles to gather all the cattle together and drive the whole herd back to Eurystheus. Once he had set out, Hera again tried to prevent the completion of the task. She sent a vicious gad-fly which bit the cattle. This made them wild with irritation. Shaking their heads madly, they ran off in all directions, scattering far and wide. It took a full year for Heracles to round them up and lead them in a straggling dusty line to the court of King Eurystheus.

With great relief, after this long and wearying journey, Heracles once more faced the king who had set the difficult task. King Eurystheus stared down from his throne as Heracles solemnly announced that he had completed his ten Labours and was ready for some rest.

The Eleventh Labour – The Apples of the Hesperides

Heracles thought that after he had delivered the cattle of Geryon to Eurystheus his Labours were completed.

But now King Eurystheus revealed what he had been secretly thinking for a long time. He claimed that only eight out of the ten Labours had been properly completed and went on to explain why.

Eurystheus had made it clear that the task of killing the Hydra should be performed 'single-handed'. As Heracles had been helped by his nephew, Iolaus, when he carried out this Labour, Eurystheus said it did not count. Also, because Heracles had demanded a reward for cleaning the Augean stables and had again been helped by Iolaus, King Eurystheus regarded that as cheating. He ruled that the Fifth Labour did not count either.

The king told Heracles sternly that he could not rest. He commanded him to perform two more Labours.

For his eleventh Labour Heracles was sent to fetch fruit from the golden apple tree in the garden of the Hesperides which lay on the slopes of Mount Atlas.

The mountain was named after a Titan called Atlas. The Titans were very early gods who existed before Zeus and the other gods who lived on Mount Olympus. In an ancient battle Zeus and his fellow gods had defeated the Titans. After this, Atlas was condemned for ever to hold up the world on his shoulders.

The garden on Mount Atlas belonged to Hera. She also owned the golden tree on which apples grew, having planted it herself. She had commanded the daughters of Atlas, who were named the Hesperides, to guard it for her.

One day she found that the Hesperides were stealing apples from the tree. As they could not be trusted, she set a fierce dragon called Ladon to coil itself around the tree and protect the fruit.

King Eurystheus was delighted with himself. Knowing that Hera disliked Heracles and that the apples were heavily guarded, he thought that at last he had found a task which it would be impossible for Heracles to complete.

The first challenge for Heracles was actually to find the garden of the Hesperides. He learnt that the one person who could give him directions and advice was a sea-god named Nereus. But first of all he had to capture Nereus who lived in the water and had the ability to change size and shape.

Heracles was lucky. Two friendly nymphs (beautiful young female goddesses) showed him where Nereus lay sleeping. Heracles crept up on the unsuspecting god and locked his arms in a wrestling hold. Promptly waking, Nereus immediately changed his shape into a sea creature with slimy tentacles. But Heracles was an expert wrestler and the old sea god was no match for a strong man. Heracles clung tenaciously onto Nereus despite the sea god's twisting and turning as again and again he changed his shape taking the form of many amazing underwater animals. Never once did Heracles relax his grip on the squirming, slippery sea creatures which Nereus became, so that eventually the cunning old sea god became totally exhausted.

Having been fairly defeated in a long wrestling match, Nereus developed enormous respect for Heracles. He gave him not only directions to the garden of the Hesperides but also some advice. He pointed out that Heracles would never be able to pick the apples himself as they were guarded closely. Instead he suggested that Heracles asked the father of the Hesperides, Atlas, to collect the fruit.

Heracles travelled onwards until at last he met Atlas. He found him, bent almost double, holding the world on his back.

After greeting Atlas, he politely asked him to do a favour and pick apples from the golden tree inside the garden. Atlas replied he was very willing to help in this way but was afraid he would be attacked by Ladon, the fierce dragon. On hearing this, Heracles strode away until he reached the garden wall. He leant over and fired a single shot from his bow. It was deadly accurate and had such force that it pierced the leathery skin of the dragon. Ladon fell dead against the tree trunk.

Atlas still hesitated, claiming there was another problem. How could he pluck the apples from the tree while he was carrying the world on his back? He asked Heracles to shoulder his burden for him while he went to the garden. He knew that Heracles possessed superhuman strength and that no one else would be capable of doing what he asked.

Accordingly Heracles bent his back and accepted the transfer of the enormous globe which Atlas gently passed to him. Straightening up and with a new spring in his step, Atlas quickly set off to the garden of his daughters, the Hesperides.

Heracles waited patiently. His neck and shoulders ached agonisingly with the weight of the world. He yearned for relief.

After what seemed like a very long time, Atlas appeared once more, bringing with him three pieces of shiny, plump, smooth fruit.

"Here are the apples from the golden tree," he announced. "You told me that they had to be taken to King Eurystheus. I have a really good idea. I will take them to him myself!"

Heracles was worried by what he heard, but he simply smiled and tried to disguise his alarm. He had been warned by Nereus that Atlas might try to trick him. Thinking quickly, he responded with care.

"Very well," he replied calmly. "I will indeed be grateful if you can carry these wonderful apples to King Eurystheus. It will save me the journey. But I must ask you first to do me another favour. I am very uncomfortable and scared that, unless I shift position, I will drop the globe. That would be a disaster for all the people of the earth. Can you please take the world back for a moment while I move slightly and adjust my cloak?"

Not clever enough to realise his own trick was being turned against him, Atlas readily agreed. He put down the apples and once more bowed his back.

Carefully Heracles transferred the globe back to Atlas.

As soon as the movement was complete, Heracles snatched up the apples. Then he turned and waved farewell, leaving Atlas to hold the world for evermore.

King Eurystheus was most surprised to see Heracles when he returned. He gazed at the apples from the golden tree but was worried about taking them because he was afraid that he would be punished by Hera. He remembered that, after all, the apples were her property. He therefore gave them back to Heracles who in turn handed them to the friendly goddess, Athene, as he too did not wish to anger Hera any further by keeping her precious apples.

Hera herself remained distraught because Heracles had killed her dragon, Ladon. She set its image among the stars as the constellation of the Serpent.

The Twelfth Labour – The Capture of Cerberus

King Eurystheus was now more determined than ever to set a task which Heracles would find impossible. This was his last chance to devise something fiendishly and frighteningly difficult.

After a great deal of thought, he commanded Heracles to capture the dog named Cerberus, which guarded the gates of the Underworld. Many people had heard tales of this creature. It was well known that Cerberus possessed three heads. Around each head, rather like a lion's mane, was coiled a fierce serpent.

After being given this task Heracles felt very sorrowful. He did not look forward to travelling to the Underworld, a distant place deep in the earth where the ghosts of the dead were believed to exist.

Before he could be allowed both to travel to, and return from, the land of the dead, it was necessary for Heracles to take part in a secret ceremony known as the Eleusinian Mysteries. Firstly he sacrificed a sow to the goddess Persephone, Queen of the Underworld, having washed it thoroughly in a sacred river. Next he had to be purified by a priest. He was blindfolded and then exposed to air, fire and water. This was just the start. There were many further rituals to be observed but no one knows exactly how they were carried out as all taking part swore a strict oath of secrecy.

Although he was now ready to depart, Heracles was still worried. He begged his father, Zeus, to help him. Answering the anxious prayers from his son, Zeus asked Athene to comfort Heracles. He also sent Hermes, the messenger of the gods, to guide him.

Led by Hermes, Heracles travelled to the banks of the River Styx, which acted like a moat, separating the land of the living from the Underworld. The ferryman, Charon, who carried the dead across the river into the Underworld, was waiting for him. So worried was Heracles that he approached with a terrible scowl upon his face. Charon had never met anyone with such a terrifying expression and trembled at the sight. Normally he demanded a coin as his ferry charge, but Charon was so afraid of the menacing appearance of Heracles that he dared not ask for payment. This was the only time anyone ever crossed the River Styx without paying!

Almost immediately Heracles stepped into the Underworld he was scared that he would die. The first thing he saw was the Gorgon, Medusa. Anyone who looked on her face was immediately turned to stone. But

Hermes reassured him. He pointed out that what Heracles was seeing was simply the ghost of Medusa, who had been slain by Perseus. The petrifying power of her eyes existed only while she was alive.

Gazing down the dark passageways, Heracles saw the ghosts of many famous people. He was frequently distracted but, having been shown the way by Hermes, he continued on his strange and frightening journey. At last he found Hades, the God of the Underworld, seated on his dark throne with the goddess Persephone at his side.

Kneeling in front of Hades, Heracles explained why he had been given ten Labours to carry out and why King Eurystheus had given him two more. He begged Hades to let him take Cerberus back to Eurystheus and so bring the final Labour to a successful conclusion.

Hades looked at him and said sternly, "Very well. I will allow you to take the dog but on one condition."

Heracles shuddered, expecting something extremely difficult. He was relieved when Hades spoke further.

"You must not use your club or your bow and arrows," Hades announced.

By his side, Persephone nodded in agreement.

These were terms which posed no problem to a man of strength. Heracles was happy to accept. He set off again back through the dark passages of the Underworld towards the set of gates near which Cerberus was kept secure with chains.

As a guard dog, Cerberus would wag his tail to welcome new arrivals into the Underworld. After all they were stepping into the realm in which they were to remain for eternity. But should unhappy ghosts try to escape, Cerberus turned savage and set about them, biting and snarling, his serpent heads lashing out to attack them.

Keeping his promise, Heracles approached Cerberus without weapons. Then, once he came close, he reached out as if to pat the dog. But at the last minute he thrust his strong hands towards the neck of Cerberus and gripped it firmly. He squeezed upon the throat of the guard dog and held on. The vicious serpents around the beast's head sprang at Heracles, hissing and biting. But, as he had done since the completion of his first Labour, Heracles was wearing the thick, impenetrable skin of the Nemean lion. Against this tough hide, serpent fangs could make no impression. Still Heracles squeezed upon the windpipe of Cerberus even though the dog kicked and twisted. Tighter and tighter became his grip until finally Cerberus choked and fell limp onto the ground.

Taking care that he did not squeeze to the last gasp, as his task was simply to capture the guard dog of the Underworld, Heracles relaxed his grip. Then he slung Cerberus over his back and hastened to leave. With Hermes to guide him, Heracles left the Underworld, once more crossing the River Styx back to the land of the living and to safety.

King Eurystheus was amazed to see Heracles back in his court. It was almost unheard of for someone to return from the land of the dead. Being a cowardly man, Eurystheus was also terrified at the sight of Cerberus. He trembled as each of the dog's three heads snarled and the serpents around its necks hissed menacingly. For the final time Eurystheus hid inside his bronze urn.

From there he shouted out to Heracles. He gave no word of congratulation but begged Heracles to return the fierce Cerberus to the underworld.

Heracles shouted back that he would do exactly that. Then, with Cerberus still slung across his shoulders, he insisted that King Eurystheus give him a binding promise. The frightened king immediately agreed and, shouting from his urn, confirmed that Heracles had completed his tasks.

The Labours of Heracles were finally over.

Heracles' Later Life

After completion of his twelve Labours, Heracles had many further adventures.

During one of these he decided to return to the Augean Stables. He remained angry with King Eurystheus who had decided that the fifth Labour had not been properly carried out. He also remained angry with King Augeias who had broken his promise to hand over one tenth of his cattle.

Heracles took with him his brother, Iphicles, who as a baby many years earlier, he had saved from Hera's serpents. As Augeas still refused to keep his promise, Heracles demanded that he abdicate as king and hand his throne over to his son. When Augeias did not agree, Heracles declared war on him.

A short but fierce battle took place. In this Heracles suffered a sad loss. Although Augeias was overthrown and Heracles was victorious, Iphicles, who was not immortal, perished. He was killed in the fighting by a pair of fierce twins known as the Moliones who, throughout their lives, were joined together at the hip.

After this battle Heracles married once again. In time his wife, Deianira, bore two children.

In his life with Deianira Heracles enjoyed much happiness and also much sadness. At one point he suffered from another fit of madness and, while deranged, killed a guest at his dinner table. For this he was banished and had to travel far away from his home. In the course of his wanderings he was drawn into many fights and displayed many feats of strength.

Heracles also joined a band of warriors brought together by another famous Greek hero, Jason. Their task was to bring back the Golden Fleece from Colchis. The heroes sailed on a ship named the Argo and, taking their name from this vessel, were called Argonauts. It was while travelling on this voyage that Jason found the few remaining birds who had escaped when Heracles cleared them from the River Stymphalia during his sixth Labour.

Sadly towards the end of his life on earth Heracles suffered great pain. Deianira had woven a colourful new robe for him to wear. Over this she poured what she had been told was a love potion. But the liquid was poisonous. It burnt Heracles' skin so that he cried out and writhed in agony. The only release was for him was the destruction of his mortal remains. His men built an enormous funeral pyre which consumed his body, scarred and scored by the poison. His spirit flew up to Mount Olympus where he lived for ever with his father Zeus and the other gods.

The stories of his Twelve Labours became known all over ancient Greece and the name Heracles became famous. Eventually the tales were written down which is why they are known and retold to this day.

Acknowledgements

My thanks must first of all go to my grandchildren who enjoy stories and inspire me to tell them. I am also grateful to one of my grandsons, Harry, for the drawing of the Nemean Lion on page 25.

I showed my first draft to fellow author Tony Corbin who made some perceptive comments and gave some helpful suggestions. Thereafter he has given constant support in this enterprise, patiently reviewing subsequent iterations. I am very grateful for his assistance.

My thanks also go to colleagues in my Basingstoke writing group, Writers Inc. They have seen selected passages and given me both suggestions and encouragement.

As ever enormous thanks go to my wife, Christine, for painstaking proof reading and general assistance in transforming a manuscript into a book.

I have known these tales since my schooldays but for completeness I have referred extensively to my copy of the classic work 'The Greek Myths' by Robert Graves.

Also by Stephen Bibby

Collingwood's Club

A Ransom for Rhodes

The Cube and the Crew: 2222

All available online from www.amazon.co.uk

Collingwood's Club

By Stephen Bibby

International financial trader, Ben Turner, secures the big bonus. Life is looking good as he is accepted into the world of the rich and powerful. Befriended by the authoritative Crispin Collingwood, Ben is sent on an assignment to South America. What he discovers there shocks him profoundly. Back in London and faced with looming crises, both financial and personal, he is forced to re-evaluate his life. He makes a brave decision to return overseas, changing not only his own destiny but also the lives of those whose fate becomes tied to his. Birth, death, love, betrayal and courage all play their part as Ben heads for a final fateful encounter.

A Ransom for Rhodes

By Stephen Bibby

A late-night phone call, a hazardous cross-country drive, and former financial trader, Ben Turner, finds himself once again lured into a society he thought he had left behind. Some two years after his terrifying ordeal in New York he has made a successful life for himself. Suddenly his comfortable existence is disrupted. Tricked into a fresh encounter with the all commanding Crispin Collingwood, he has no option but to undertake a mission beset with difficulties. A journey to Africa brings danger to himself and his family as he confronts duplicity, greed and treachery. But is all what it seems and can he succeed when faced with ruthless opponents?

The Cube and the Crew: 2222

By Stephen Bibby

It is the year 2222 and the spacecraft "Odysseus" is on a mission to discover alien life.

But what is the curious object Captain Heathwood Bede has discovered on board and what is the true identity of his secretive First Lieutenant?

Join the crew as they hurtle through galaxies unknown, encountering perils undreamt of. Billions of miles from Earth, how will they respond to unexpected challenges and, as their adventure reaches its climax, how will they resolve an unwelcome dilemma?

This is an exciting novel aimed at younger readers written especially for the author's grandchildren.

Printed in Great Britain
by Amazon